For Cathy Freese

All rights reserved. Published in the United States by Houghton Mifflin Harcourt
Publishing Company. Originally published in hardcover in the United States by Clarion
Books, an imprint of Houghton Mifflin Harcourt Publishing Company, 1985.

For information about permission to reproduce selections from this book, write to trade.
permissions@hmhco.com or to Permissions, Houghton Mifflin Harcourt Publishing
Company, 3 Park Avenue, 19th Floor, New York, New York 10016.

www.hmhco.com

The Library of Congress Cataloging-in-Publication data is on file.

ISBN: 978-0-89919-336-6 hardcover
ISBN: 978-0-89919-705-0 paperback
ISBN: 978-0-547-38946-2 paper over board

Manufactured in China
SCP 10 9 8 7 6 5 4 3 2 1

4500634370

Cat Goes Fiddle-i-fee

Adapted and Illustrated by
PAUL GALDONE

HOUGHTON MIFFLIN HARCOURT
Boston   New York

I had a cat and the cat pleased me,
I fed my cat by yonder tree.

Cat goes fiddle-i-fee.

I had a hen and the hen pleased me,
I fed my hen by yonder tree.

Hen goes chimmy-chuck, chimmy-chuck,
Cat goes fiddle-i-fee.

I had a duck and the duck pleased me,
I fed my duck by yonder tree.

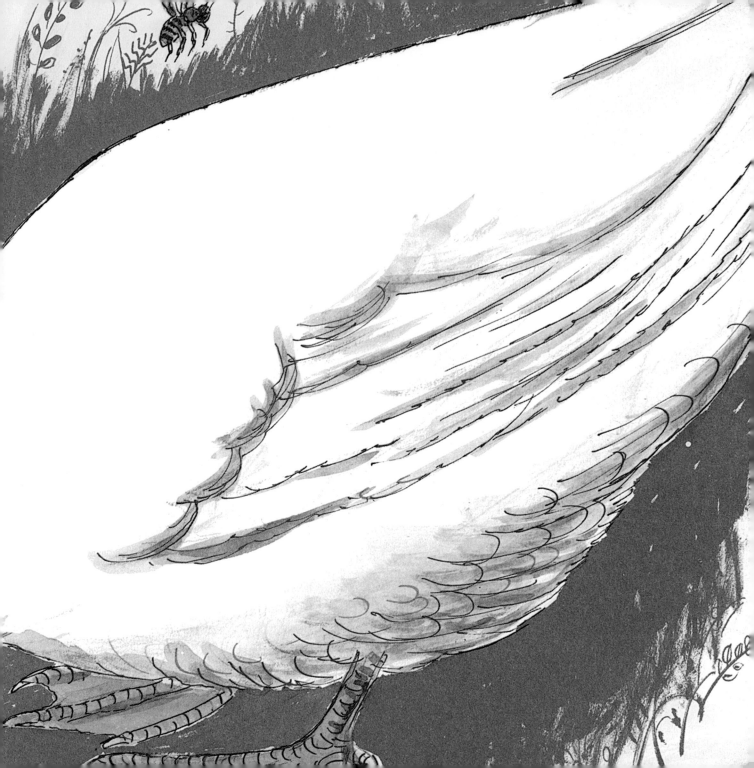

Duck goes quack, quack,
Hen goes chimmy-chuck, chimmy-chuck,
Cat goes fiddle-i-fee.

I had a goose and the goose pleased me,
I fed my goose by yonder tree.

Goose goes swishy, swashy,
Duck goes quack, quack,
Hen goes chimmy-chuck, chimmy-chuck,
Cat goes fiddle-i-fee.

I had a sheep and the sheep pleased me,
I fed my sheep by yonder tree.

Sheep goes baa, baa,
Goose goes swishy, swashy,
Duck goes quack, quack,
Hen goes chimmy-chuck, chimmy-chuck,
Cat goes fiddle-i-fee.

I had a pig and the pig pleased me,
I fed my pig by yonder tree.

Pig goes griffy, gruffy,
Sheep goes baa, baa,
Goose goes swishy, swashy,
Duck goes quack, quack,
Hen goes chimmy-chuck, chimmy-chuck,
Cat goes fiddle-i-fee.

I had a cow and the cow pleased me,
I fed my cow by yonder tree.

Cow goes moo, moo,
Pig goes griffy, gruffy,
Sheep goes baa, baa,
Goose goes swishy, swashy,
Duck goes quack, quack,
Hen goes chimmy-chuck, chimmy-chuck,
Cat goes fiddle-i-fee.

I had a horse and the horse pleased me,
I fed my horse by yonder tree.

Horse goes neigh, neigh,
Cow goes moo, moo,
Pig goes griffy, gruffy,
Sheep goes baa, baa,
Goose goes swishy, swashy,
Duck goes quack, quack,
Hen goes chimmy-chuck, chimmy-chuck,
Cat goes fiddle-i-fee.

I had a dog and the dog pleased me,
I fed my dog by yonder tree.

Dog goes bow-wow, bow-wow,
Horse goes neigh, neigh,
Cow goes moo, moo,
Pig goes griffy, gruffy,
Sheep goes baa, baa,
Goose goes swishy, swashy,
Duck goes quack, quack,
Hen goes chimmy-chuck, chimmy-chuck,
Cat goes fiddle-i-fee.

Then Grandma came
and she fed me…

while the others dozed
by yonder tree.

And cat went fiddle-i-fee.